A BEAR TO SHARE

written by **Jessica Alba,**
Norah Weinstein, and **Kelly Sawyer Patricof**

illustrated by Alicia Más

HARPER

An Imprint of HarperCollinsPublishers

To Honor, Haven, Hayes, and all the kind little souls out there, keep shining bright —JA

For Riley & Sawyer and Orange Ted, and children everywhere —KSP

For Sloane & Graham, their bears, Teddy & Carmy, and every child
who deserves a bear of their own —NW

Special thanks to Jamie, Pete, and Luana.

A Bear to Share
Copyright © 2021 by Temple Hill Publishing, Kelly Sawyer Patricof, and Norah Weinstein
Illustrations by Alicia Más
All rights reserved. Manufactured in Italy.
No part of this book may be used or reproduced in any manner whatsoever without written
permission except in the case of brief quotations embodied in critical articles and reviews.
For information address HarperCollins Children's Books, a division of
HarperCollins Publishers, 195 Broadway, New York, NY 10007.
www.harpercollinschildrens.com

ISBN 978-0-06-295717-7

Typography by Chelsea C. Donaldson
21 22 23 24 25 RTLO 10 9 8 7 6 5 4 3 2 1
❖
First Edition

As the co-CEOs and an ambassador of Baby2Baby, we know that no child should be without clean diapers, clothing, food, toys, and more. But the reality is millions of families cannot afford even the most basic necessities for their children.

That's why the mission of Baby2Baby is to provide children living in poverty with the essentials they all deserve. Since 2011, we've distributed over 175 million items to children in need. All the generous people and companies who donate money, time, and items make it possible for Baby2Baby to serve over a million children across the country.

And it's not just grown-ups who can make a difference. The good news for kids is you're never too young to start giving back! You will see that something magical happens when you give something that you love to someone who needs it more than you.

This book is a dream come true for us because teaching kids to give back has always been such an important part of Baby2Baby. *A Bear to Share* is a story about a young girl named Tiana who proves that even a small gesture of generosity and kindness can have a big impact. We hope that Tiana inspires you to help people and children in your community by giving back in any way you can!

With love,
Jessica, Norah & Kelly

Tiana loved her teddy bear.
His name was Bach the Bear. And he was
absolutely, positively perfect.

Bach was the only bear for her. There was a lot that made Bach special.

He had one eye because when Tiana was little, she carried him around by the eyeball until one day it popped clean off. But she didn't mind.

His fur was worn down from Tiana holding him close to her heart.
But she still thought he was soft and cuddly.

He had stuffing coming out of his neck. Tiana didn't
actually know *why* he had stuffing coming out of his neck.
But it gave him **pizzazz.**

In fact, she named him Bach the Bear because when Tiana placed him on top of her toy piano, he made every note sound better.

They lived together in perfect harmony.

Then one day, without any warning at all, Tiana's mom yelled, "**Surprise!** Look what Aunt Maria got you. She thought you'd love a new bear."

Tiana *didn't* understand.

"But Mom, what about Bach?"

"Honey, I know you love Bach, but don't you think it's time to make room for another bear? Bach has one eye, his fur is all worn down, and he's all . . . well . . . unstuffed."

Tiana looked at Bach the Bear.

Then she looked at the new bear.

He had both his eyes, he was fluffy, and he was *super* stuffed.

It did make her wonder. . . .

Tiana woke up for school and couldn't wait to talk to her best friend, Timothy.

She spotted him on the monkey bars immediately because Timothy was wearing the same overalls he wears most days. Timothy was the best climber on the playground. Luckily, he was the best listener too, because this was an **emergency!**

"You won't **BELIEVE** what my mom said,"
Tiana started to explain to him.

Timothy, like Tiana, didn't understand either.

"I guess Mom thinks Bach is too old and worn out.
Maybe she thinks he's lost his music."

"Well . . . I've never had a teddy bear, so
Bach always seemed pretty great to me."

Tiana was shocked. "Why don't you just ask your parents for a teddy bear?" she asked.

"They say we can't afford it. Toys aren't a **pri-o-ri-ty.**" Timothy said every part of the last word very carefully while looking down at his shoes.

For the first time ever, Tiana didn't know what to say.
She wished Timothy could have a teddy bear too.

"Mom," Tiana said when they were on their way home, "did you know Timothy has never, ever, ever, ever had a teddy bear?"

"You know, we're very lucky," Mom said. "We have enough money
to take care of you and some left over for nice things, like toys."

"It's not fair that I have two bears and
Timothy has **zero** bears," Tiana said.

"All families are different, honey. Some have less, some have more, and some have just enough," Mom said holding Tiana's hands softly. "And although things can be unfair and unequal, it doesn't mean we can't do something about it."

Tiana finally started to understand.

She looked at Bach carefully.
He only had one eye because she loved him so much.
His fur was all worn down because she loved him so much.
His stuffing was coming out of his neck—she still didn't
know why—but she still loved him so much.

Then Tiana had an idea. A big idea . . .

"Mom, what if we give Timothy the new bear? Even if he's old and used up, Bach is *my* bear."

Tiana knew Timothy deserved a bear to love and make his own. One with both of its eyes and all of its stuffing so he could feel as special as she did when she got Bach.

Her mom smiled at her. "I love that idea, baby girl!"

When Tiana gave Timothy the new teddy bear, he looked so happy. It was like a candle lit up inside him making him shine. It made Tiana feel like she was shining too. Like she had received a gift, instead of giving one.

Timothy named the bear Billie because he loves jazz.
The new bear was Timothy's perfect match . . .

. . . and they all played together
in **perfect harmony.**